Makes Murky Waters Sparkle

E. I. Karnes

MAKES MURKY WATERS SPARKLE. Copyright © 2014, 2015, 2017, 2020, 2021; cover photography and design—published by E. I. Karnes
Editor-in-chief: M. W. Karnes
Copyeditor: M. A. Meholick
Published 2022. All rights reserved.
Second Edition

ISBN: 979-8-218-01198-7

Library of Congress Control Number: 2022909870

Pine Grove
Pennsylvania

Other Work
by E. I. Karnes, et al.
—Pushing Poetry—

Pushing Poetry articulates perception of nature, wander and inquisitions of reality.

The graphic rhythm of each poem elucidates its own aesthetic escapade, often describing existence and the adversities that inevitably occur once entangled in living, while the perseverance and gratitude manifest at its inception sparks the desire to continue forward as the discord thickens.

PLEASE READ

Thank You So Much to those standing by me today who all believed that I would prevail over what my darkest days illuminated.

Contents
Makes Murky Waters Sparkle

Lost Your Way?   01
The Hitchhiker   02
Friday, Aug. 29, 2014 at 6:10 p.m.   03
Restraints   04
House of Trees   05
My Mafia   06
Pornography   07
Saturday-Night Blues   08
Naturalist   09
Envy   10
Mission Accomplished   11
"For Someone New"   12
If Only I Were Wrong   13
A Leg   14
Main Street   15
Aliens in the Closet   16
This Is Why   17
Odds & Beginnings   18
Asylum   19
Questions   20
Lies   21
Like I'm Yours   22
Not the Blues   23
Going Dutch   24
I Won't Miss You   25
Here Comes the Rain   26
Listen Dylan   27
Chess   28
Last Year   29
Things Have Changed   30
In the Beginning   31

The Ride Away   32

Blackjack   33

I'm Not In Love (Anymore)   34

The Stand   35

Gone Like the Wind   36

Song   37

Dates   38

Relations   39

Appearances   41

The Wave Away   42

Walk Away   43

Bassinet On the Doorstep   44

What I Feel Inside   45

Feels Like What?   46

Monopoly   47

Newfangled Company Store   48

The Golden Door   49

I Love You   50

Sun Is Bright   51

Flowers For You, Too   52

Mother Bear   53

Mixed Thoughts   54

Nothing Less   55

Traveling Blues   56

The Jack in Pandora's Box   57

Words   58

Insomnia   59

Goldfish   60

Nighttime Balance   61

Defeating Purposes   62

Incorrigibles   63

New Beginnings   64

Witch   65

Slide   66

Again   67

Upon Time   68
Dreaming   69
Trees Eat Themselves   70
For Life   71
Filler   72
Viewing   73
Portrait   74
Misconception?   75
Looking On   76
Reciprocate   77
Breeze   78
It Was the Same   79
Closing Mind   80
Lost My Way   81
Compulsion   82
Reoccurrence Hill   83

ENJOY

Lost Your Way?

Have you ever tried to kill
Yourself from the inside:
Your mind a broken piece of glass,
Blood splattered upon the shield?

Have you ever broken down and
Shattered a bone from the inside?

Have you ever lost your way?

The Hitchhiker

There was a guy on the road.
"Somebody help me."

I look into the rearview. What do I see there?
"Somebody save me."

Slip and slide on the same road.
"Somebody kill me."

All in the same cell, sell me to the devil.
Compulsion is the buyer.

Soft asylum release me:
Kill what's inside of me.

Friday, Aug. 29, 2014 at 6:10 p.m.

The line has been drawn
With paint on
A wet road.
Devastation
Rounds the corner and
Slides into fourth
Only to finish first.

Restraints

Don't make me have to use the pigs on the farm.
Don't make me have to walk through the fuzz.
I want you gone.
You want to know why?
Just because.
Don't place in danger or touch those I know close.
Don't make me see you if blood runs its course
As my face to face will end you once my ties are knotted.

House of Trees

Don't come back to my door.
I don't want to see you anymore,
Knowing who you are.

Welcome back and to leave.
Your mind is broken go and see
Or close your eyes.

Welcome back to my door.
You've been naked once before:
You need no clothes to hide.

You got into something,
You need to get out, but the
Truth is you don't know how.

It might get real,
Run fast—go.
I'll go for the kill.

My Mafia

He thinks that he can get away,
But he can't get away—
He can't get away from my mafia.

I speak to my friends,
I speak to myself,
I speak to my mother and
I speak to heaven itself:
I speak to myself.

That's our government.
The conspiracy is against my mafia—
Against my own business.

"You know where to come.
Call me on the phone. We'll have fun,"
The girl on the street says.

Pornography

"Stick 'em up!" she yells, 9 mm in her wiry hand.
Compliant the man's penis starts to harden.
Upon full erection he is scared stiff.
She surmounts his dick.

Saturday-Night Blues

"The dream's come true and
I'm running from you and
I can't get it out of my soul.

It's been a long time since
I've cared this much and
I can't get it out of my soul."

'This is me.
They're coming for me and
I don't know where I should go.

It's been like this for a long,
Long time and
Don't know who I should know.'

"Trying to find my way back to
This life that wasn't unto you.

Trying to find my way back to
Dreams come true."

Naturalist

One evening there was this boy who determined that the music around him from the bug world had the most beautiful lyrics of any song he had ever heard.

The girl next to him could only hear wings in the wind and did not understand any of the words.

The girl was so envious of all the love that the boy interpreted from the music that her heart was off beat to the pulse in the boy's hand that held hers.

The girl could only see herself as the tears blocked her view of the world and so she cried more until she was so blinded that there were no eyes to even look upon.

Envy

Monster of green
Distorts our dreams,
So it seems.

Mission Accomplished

Come on.
Why won't you relax
For me?

Let's take ourselves out
To the shore.

In my eyes changes.

Come on.
Why won't you help
Me out?

Never say
It is OK.

What is wrong with you?

"For Someone New"

'Why won't you kiss me today?
Why won't you see me again?
You're gone like the wind.'

"Can't control: you're playing me today,
Can't let the water wash it away."

'You're gone like the wind,
Beyond my control.'

"Seeing you, hearing things you say:
Life wasn't meant to be this way."

'You're gone like the wind,
Beyond my control,
Like a fire burning in this long-lost soul.'

If Only I Were Wrong

I admit an untruthful wrong
To see how far it will go and
If it will even be taken.

The lie weighs heavy on my heart
As it elates your mistaken mind
Yet I continue to play up to your faults.

Relying on you to make a correction
Stunts our connection
So we go in separate directions
As you take my confession further.

Testing the depth of your mind
I find it is shallow and
Rather than embark
In confrontation
I seek other relations.

A Leg

I would have stepped further, but
Your trap has me caught. I am now idle.
Deciding to move I release the grasp of the trap, but
Now my body is no longer whole.
I have left something for you:
I limp and stumble away bleeding.

Main Street

Before I knew where I was going
I went through town.
I stopped to ask a question and
I got shot down.

I called on my friends
Who I took to the end.
They said I was worth nothing and
They wouldn't let me in.

I've been thrown out on the highway.
I've been thrown out on the road.
I've been thrown out on Main Street,
My god: no covenant, no code.

I've been working on helium,
I've been working on balloons,
I've been doing my homework:
I've got nothing to lose.

Aliens in the Closet

Much scarier than your own bones
Your mind searches for something that should be known
Yet you keep it hidden from your own soul.

Cutting through your skin
You see blood rise to the surface.
Understanding that you cut too deep
You still let the blood seep.

As those who pretend to see
Beyond the color of your eyes
You still maintain face by standing by society: disgrace.
When are you going to break out?

Stop running at everyone else's pace.
You already know
How your own blood tastes.

This Is Why

Warm blood runs red;
It's dark and cold dead.

Odds & Beginnings

This stuff is not going to mean much to me soon.

So to you I give—
These I hand.

Marks like ink under the surface sink.
Presence of memories and what of and how you think.

No different than putting it on paper
Or sand over glass: sunsets, skulls and names of the past.

Asylum

I'm going someplace slow,
Not far from my life on the go.

I'm going to get the breeze to flow
Through my fingers
As my hair is pulled back
Away from the past.

I am going to travel low,
My life on the highroad
Has broken down.

As I fall I hope
It's not too difficult
To get back up.

Questions

What's the secret?
What's it doing in your mind?
Why won't you share?

Lies

It's too hard to remember.
The thoughts—they are all torn and thrown together.
They're all plated.

Like I'm Yours

It's time I behave like I am yours.
Rely on you,
Not cheat on you,
Not fuck your friends
Like I do.

It's time I behave like you.
Kissing you and
Loving you and
Cherishing all that you do.
Dressing up and kissing up and
Never really fucking up.

It's time I behave like you.
Calling you:
I'll be late.
Not staying out on a date,
Not swinging by your favorite place
Like I do without you.

It's time I behave like you.
Buying rings and
Singing songs and
Crying
When I kiss you wrong.

It's time I behave like I am yours.

Not the Blues

No matter what I do first,
Play with you,
Make them feel worse.

Carry on what we all do.
Just be happy,
It's just me and you.

How many do you all do?
Lie to me,
But I know it's true.

Take what you know and
Pass it on please, just be sure
You're the only one for me.

When you go I hope I didn't lose
What's in my purse?
I hope it's not the blues.

Going Dutch

I am today,
Listen to what I have
To say,

I hope you read the text this way:
Love it, fuck it—
There're other days.

Hold on,
We're gonna see,
Words you hear are not real.

Sorry 'bout it,
Kick me out,
I guess we'll never really find out.

Love me, hold me,
This way sucks;
Catch me before

I come too much.
Love me, hold me,
Let's go Dutch.

I Won't Miss You

They'll come back for me.
Want more of me?
They'll want more of me,
Come back for me.

Feel me up and
Go down on me,
Follow my lead in,
No more bleeding.

I want you
Only when I want you,
I want you
Only when I need you.

Here Comes the Rain

Never loved anybody.
Never loved you before.
Why should I start now?
You walk out the door.

Here comes the rain
Washing you away.
Look at you loving me,
Cry a little more.

Never loved anybody.
Never loved you before.
Why should I start now?
You left me before.

Listen Dylan

Been called a lot of things.
These sticks and stones
Have hurt my bones:
Called a lot of things.

Listen Dylan,
I've nowhere to go.
The men on my mind
Are coming back in time.

Forget the world
You've nowhere to go,
Far away you're just another blow.
Watch out baby, I'm coming slow.

Called a lot of things.

Chess

The only rule to the game I play is your heart and
Every move I make I am breaking it apart.

You are the most important
Being that my life has ever known.

Please help my knowledge grow,
Let me be a part of who you are and your soul.

Give me another chance: I won't harm, destroy
Or play it like a toy.

I will cherish what is given to me
In an ever longing to be true.

Last Year

Happy times have brought me here.
Maybe last year I had a few more.
When I met you I thought I knew
How to treat me like I treat you.

Been down for a while.
Had a few more than last year.
Couldn't count on you, you weren't around
To pick me up off the ground,

You weren't around.

Things Have Changed

Sometimes in the night I hear you cry,
Tears of what you keep inside.

You in my life things have changed,
All that I've wanted: nothing's the same.

There is no game that you play with me
Because things aren't the same as they used to be.

In the Beginning

As satisfying as it is to have you on my mind and
Wanting you in such a way
That I can no longer conclude my thoughts and
Really wanting us to be holding each other and
Sharing each breath,

I am afraid.

At the end of the day, when we are apart,
I have so many worries that have to do with my heart.

Maybe it has never been completely intact,

But if you were to keep me
I wouldn't know
How many pieces it is capable of making and

At the same time hoping it only falls in two
When the time comes all too soon.

The Ride Away

To see you walk away, head down as I stay,
I know in my heart, empty as it might seem,
Hurting even as I dream,

We are always meant to be together.
As I repeat the last line, over and over, and

As it echoes I know I am lying.
You were my life my love.
I drive away, inside crying.

Blackjack

It's a weird day in paradise.
We played a game of roll the dice.
Your choice, your number—single.
My choice of two no match for you.
You would not reach higher.

Playing a game on opposing teams
You win.
Strength in numbers
No wonder one gets under.

Don't play with me.
Play and you will see.
The cost is much too high.
My two out of your price.

Your game has just begun.
I've paid my fare now I'm done.
With you now I am one.

Beyond you
I do
See a two.

I'm Not In Love (Anymore)

I'm not crying anymore.
I'm not locking my door.
I'm not seeing clouds
Any different then I did before.
I'm not in love anymore.

When you come knocking on my door
I won't see you anymore.
I don't want you coming home to me,
Just like I told you before because
I'm not in love anymore.

The Stand

I'm not going to cry anymore;
I'm not going to sleep at your door.
I'm done sleeping in the cold.

Why have you treated me like a puppy on a leash?
Tug me down one more time and I'll drown.

Sometimes it's best to run while you can.
Sometimes it's best to hide.
Might be best to stand.

I'm not going to sing your song anymore.
I can't carry your key.

Why have you treated me so wrong of late?
Darkness is coming soon.

I'm not going to play your game anymore.
Win or lose,
My life is too precious to bruise.

Gone Like the Wind

Could never write a song about you,
Gone like the wind beside my pillow at night.

Dreamt of you, but you weren't there.
Beautiful as you are, it's hard not to care.

Won't think of you, not how you are.
Won't think about every damn last scar.

Things got expensive,
Couldn't afford who you are.

Every last dime,
All my goddamn time.

Song

So in love you tell me all the time,
Been so long and hard for me to find.
Looking for something more—the truth,
Staring at you hurt and confused.

Dates

I wait for you.
It's the last thing I do.
Counting the times that we have been together
Goes beyond my mathematical ability,
But the clock keeps time.
It's been too long.

Relations

It will only take a moment to break down this trial,
To make it real and be chill for a while.

Maybe you would better understand
If I were to sway rather than stay.

But me, I can't say no.
Not on this high, not going to lie;

I'm trapped in an hour
As if were days at a time

In this fucked-up tower
Waiting for my heroine to join me

Or take me down from this pile of shit
That I stepped in, it's no fucking ditch,

It's a ripped out heart
That I just can't fix.

I have a little something that I'd like to share.
Maybe I could call and talk to you, as if you really care.

Like I said, my words don't mean a thing and
All you bring is heartache to this ring.

My phone won't go, not even as I drive slow,
Like what I've done—only you will know

Because telling on people is a joke,
No smoke, only coke.

These days ahead are what I dread
Like these locks on my head.

I can't go out without a shout
Because all these people think that

I'm some kind of dick when they see me
Until they get a lick.

"Tastes like candy," they even lie a little bit.

On and on I can't roll no more,
I got to put out the flame to this fucking hellhole.

I've got to close the door before I die
Because leaving it open is like living in heaven,

Which I've never believed in, and as I go out
I'm screaming, 'Go fuck yourself. I'm leaving.'

Appearances

It could be a long ride.
I have the cops on my tail
Going one-30 straight to hell

And I have you on my mind
As if you were a line.

Jonesing for my next cup of coffee
I added a little sugar for appearances,
As though I really care what I blow.

The Wave Away

There are reasons for every score,
As if you disliking me makes me like you more.
As my desire is filled my heart beats hotter.
You are the goal, the coal that lights the fire.
Please be patient with me, it will only take a while
For me to put out the flames with my hand in denial.

Walk Away

If this is how my life turns out
Will they look at me the same?

Will they joust
Or just look away?

Will they call me names?

I can't help that I feel this way.
I want you regardless.

I want you the way you are,
The way you will be.

Bassinet On the Doorstep

He loves someone else and
I don't care.

That's what this is all about,
Love is to share.

I opened his eyes;
If only she knew.

That's what this is about,
Love that I gave you.

What I Feel Inside

You are what I feel inside,
An emotion in my mind.
I only breathe lies to myself
Because the truth hurts so much.

What have you done to me?

I feel so broken. Please stay and
Find the pieces that I lost,
Once you find them
You have what pieces are my heart.

Feels Like What?

It feels as if I were being put through the wash.
The cycle has me spinning—I'm sick.
It is draining. It is filling and
I am drowning.

I still feel dirty, but the cycle has not yet completed.
Once again I am filled, drained and spun.
Being hung out to dry would be the end,
But I am worn once again and

The cycle starts over.

Monopoly

Superficial thoughts wash my mind.
My body, an account, depletes
As I continue to spend from within my emotional bank.

I want for you to repossess my heart.
Biding my time I wait for your interest to accrue,
But as my mortgage increases your interest ceases.

Newfangled Company Store

Don't borrow money from them;
They're no friend of mine.
They're crooked to give and take and take
A quarter and capitalize a dime.

The Golden Door

Never thought that thought before.
Ten minutes and an open front door.

Many rings come inside,
Open up—come inside.

Turn the key patiently.
Keep in mind the gold I hide.

Runaround look in my eyes.
Can't you see the tears I've cried?

I Love You

I love you in my life.
Try and see who it is I am,
Beyond the thought,
I love you again.

I love you in my life.
Let me see who it is you are and
I will love you again,
I will love you again.

Sun Is Bright

Sun is bright in my eyes,
Crawling out of mud back in disguise.
Sun is bright in my eyes,
Back in disguise one more night,
Back in disguise one more night.

Rolling into town he brought up my name.
Sometimes life is just the same.
Brought another into his game.
He thinks that I am still the same,
That I'm still playing his game.

Flowers For You, Too

When there is nothing to do,
I'll bring flowers to you.

In case we say goodbye,
These flowers?
Well, they'll die.

Cigarettes and wine,
All will come in time.
Write a song with you in mind,
Cigarettes and wine.

Mother Bear

You love me more than I love you,
But I couldn't bear to hurt you,
So I gave into your loneliness
And said 'I do' with a single kiss.

You wouldn't return me
To the place I believe,
Beneath the darkening water,
Where my mother waits for me.

You say you love me more than I could care
So you throw me in your lonely lair and
Make me dance until
My feet are bare.

Being lost not caring where,
Wishing I were far away from you,
Wishing I were with
My Mother Bear.

Mixed Thoughts

...but never too sound,
For I see his heart beat,
It never misses a bound.

Never have I told him,
I do not want him to leave
The leashes and chains

He was brought to believe.

Nothing Less

Will this, love, keep bringing me down?

After the circus has ended
You still entreat me to a frown.

Traveling Blues

Run away from every thought
That has ever passed through your mind.

Never tried to be like you,
You pass through my mind.

Never had a dream as true
As this one without you.

You came into my life
Instead we had to leave you behind.

When it's time for me to go
I hope you know that it's true.

Pick me up where I left off and
Forgive my hidden shoes.

The Jack in Pandora's Box

Been enticed and bribed—
Not even knowing why,
How or what for.

I sold myself:
Candy for a kiss.

Smoked cigarettes and
Liked dick.

When the time came
I had no say because it wasn't only me
Being betrayed.

Words

I tear at the words within my mind,
Wondering if his soul is blind
As I express what I feel inside and
Felt at those times in my life.

Insomnia

I am the black sheep;
I am the black sheep.

No sleep for you;
No sleep for you.

Watch my white friends
Over the fence now.

No sleep for you.

Goldfish

What if I set my fish free?
Where would they be?
Swimming in the sea?

They are goldfish.

What if I set my fish free?
Where would they be
Swimming in the sea?

They are goldfish.

What if I set my fish free?
Would they be free,
Swimming in the sea?

They are goldfish.

Nighttime Balance

Watch him go:
Sinking fast,
Maybe slow.

Defeating Purposes

I am drowning and you throw me a bucket of water.
I am digging and you throw me another shovel.
I find myself and you give me a map.
I understand where you are coming from and you leave.
I understand where you are coming from and I lock the door.

Incorrigibles:

Only to be used
As steppingstones and tools.

New Beginnings

Don't make me a part of your plan.
The gate to the garden is closed.
The slipper fell from your foot.
Now I see what path I have beaten.
It has though grown over.

Witch

Sometimes things go right
When they should be left.

Why am I always slipping
When I do my best?

I realize though I do no wrong.
Mistakes count
As if I can't add and

They deduct
Because all adds up to
Death no matter what!

Slide

It takes a frame of mind.
No frame of mine:

With each whimper, seduction cries, smiles I hide.

Crossing paths with you—whoever knew
Had something else in mind
Beside the tears now behind.

Dying for an easier life.
Dying because it has been in strife.

Is this how I imagined it to be?
How it is, is just a thought away.

Again

One-lane road one way, one way out of two ways,
Single time I'm stuck again.

One day in a two day, second day, end day,
The week has come again.

Living life lonely has got to go someday.
Holding on—to cards once played.

One thought one way, one-track mind another day,
Lost in my thoughts once again.

Channel, tunnel that way, drowning in it one day,
Progress regress yesterday.

Upon Time

One thought—fast!
So close to being past.

Dreaming

When the storyline without you begins,
The paths we have been traveling,
The stars we have been gazing at,
The touches we share—
What will make me think of you?
All these things?

Trees Eat Themselves

Preservation is in memory.
There is really no end.
Molecular bodies though now only sleeping souls
Influence stories and thoughts
Of charged particles that are still creating.

For Life

As energy comes from the dead,
Stories of those gone
Might influence as if one were still in body.

Filler

Lost in metaphors.
I cannot
Make sense of—

Viewing

To be seen
With
Comfort in your eyes.

Portrait

With each expression
Being a representation of our thoughts and
In an attempt to show each other
How we view one another—

Misconception?

When you refuse
To let me see you
The way you see yourself,
How do you expect me
To show myself to you?
I die every time.

Looking On

Take down your troubles,
I am here to stare
At what you have,
What you are and
What you want to be.

I see in your eyes,
Naked in front of me.

Reciprocate

Respect me:
I will not look down upon you.
Say no to me: respect yourself.

Breeze

You bring the breeze.
Maybe one day it will bring you once again
To my door.

It Was the Same

Out in the wilderness
It was just the same
As being in lockdown.

When it struck morning
Light shown through the trees
To the bed of ground I used to lie upon
Of sticks from dying hemlocks.

A week later it was morning again,
But this time
Light shown through
The corners of the window shade.

I had credit both places,
But either place I wasn't
Merciful by the hand of my own.

Closing Mind

What the hell happened here?
I took a trip in time,
Lost it all, lost my mind,
Left my friends behind.

Closing mind. Closing mind.

I took you all for wrong.
Never did I mean to be
Hanging on too long.
Now I know where you all come from.

I saw it in my mind. I saw it in my mind.

I took a trip across the sea
Many months with you,
Then I took a day off,
It broke my heart in two.

Closing mine. Closing mine.

Lost My Way

Been gone a long time,
Gone too long,
Gone so long,
Gone too long.

Placing on the line
All that I hold dear:
Everyone near me.

Lost my way,
Lost all time—
Lost the words
On my mind,

Gone too long.

Compulsion

The hot impulse to live
Once the cold has set in
Is beyond wild remorse
For living in the first place.

Reoccurrence Hill

I keep rolling, there's no stopping me.
Lying beneath the trees dreaming of you.
I keep walking, there's no path I am following,
Lost now.

Breathing, dreaming, senses declining,
Places of hiding, dying then surviving.

Trying to escape my own mind,
The hill is the reason I survived:
Saved me from my own demise.

Driving, no brakes applying,
Flying.

You left me crying, tears falling,
So sad.

Music playing, over you not staying,
Smiling.

giggles

About the Author

E. I. Karnes resides in Pennsylvania and graduated from Penn State University with a baccalaureate from the College of Communications in Journalism.

This author is a self-proclaimed philosopher, enjoys art and working with various mediums, likes kayaking, music and volunteers much of her time helping to create and maintain an ecologically diverse and recreationally friendly environment.